OUR BURROW

HILL

THE RAINBARREL

FREE GARBIDGE

THE GARDEN

RL

EX LIBRIS

DUANE DUNKIN

Rabbit Hill

Also written and illustrated by Robert Lawson

THEY WERE STRONG AND GOOD

ROBBUT: A TALE OF TAILS

THE TOUGH WINTER

THE GREAT WHEEL

Illustrated by Robert Lawson

THE STORY OF FERDINAND

WEE GILLIS

ADAM OF THE ROAD

THE WEE MEN OF BALLYWOODEN

Rabbit Hill

by Robert Lawson

The Viking Press · New York

COPYRIGHT 1944 BY ROBERT LAWSON
FIRST PUBLISHED IN 1944 BY THE VIKING PRESS, INC.
625 MADISON AVENUE, NEW YORK 22, N. Y.
PUBLISHED IN CANADA BY
THE MACMILLAN COMPANY OF CANADA LIMITED

First published September 1944
Second printing before publication
Third printing October 1944
Fourth printing April 1945
Fifth printing October 1946
Sixth printing July 1951
Seventh printing May 1956
Eighth printing (from new plates) April 1960

PRINTED IN THE U.S.A. BY AFFILIATED LITHOGRAPHERS

For T.
who *loves*
Little Georgie

Contents

1. New Folks Coming   11

2. Mother Worries   27

3. Little Georgie Sings a Song   35

4. Uncle Analdas   51

5. Porkey Sits Tight   61

6. Moving Vans   69

7. Reading Rots the Mind   75

8. Willie's Bad Night   87

9. Dividing Night   95

10. Clouds Over the Hill   103

11. Strain and Strife   111

12. There Is Enough for All   119

Rabbit Hill

1. New Folks Coming

ALL THE Hill was boiling with excitement. On every side
there rose a continual chattering and squeaking,
whispering and whistling, as the Animals discussed the

great news. Through it all could be heard again and again the words, "New Folks coming."

Little Georgie came tumbling down the Rabbit burrow, panting out the tidings. "New Folks coming," he shouted. "New Folks coming, Mother — Father, new Folks coming into the Big House!"

Mother looked up from the very thin soup that she was stirring. "Well, it's high time there were new Folks in the Big House, *high* time, and I do hope they're planting Folks, not shiftless like the last ones. Three years now since there's been a good garden on this place. Never enough to put anything up for the winters and last winter the worst in years. I don't know how we ever got through it and I don't know how we'll ever make out if they're not planting Folks, I just don't know, with food getting scarcer all the time and no place to get a vegetable except the Fat-Man's-at-the-Crossroads, and him with his Dogs and all, and crossing the Black Road twice a day to get there. I just don't know, I just don't know—" Mother was quite a worrier.

"Now, my dear," said Father, "do try to adopt a more optimistic attitude. This news of Georgie's may promise the approach of a more felicitous and bountiful era. Perhaps it would be well if I were to indulge in a short stroll about the neighborhood and seek confirmation of this most

auspicious rumor." Father was a Southern Gentleman and
always talked like that.

As he picked his way through the long neglected garden
the big brick house loomed up dark and lonely in the twilight. It looked very gloomy, no lights in the windows,
no Folks about. The roof shingles were curled and rot-
ting, blinds hung crookedly. In the walks and driveway
tall, dried weeds rattled and scraped whenever a breeze

stirred. Now that all the earth was stirring with spring it seemed even more depressing.

There had been a time, he remembered it wistfully, when things had been quite different here on the Hill. The lawns then had been thick carpets of delicious grass, the fields heavy with clover. Garden vegetables had been plentiful; he and Mother and all their numerous offspring had lived well, all the Little Animals had lived well.

There had been good Folks there in those days, children too, who had played tag with them evenings, who had squealed with delight when mother Skunks, their little ones strung out behind in solemn Indian file, had paraded across the lawn. There had been a Dog, a lady Spaniel, old and fat, who carried on endless noisy arguments with the Woodchucks, but had never been known to harm anyone. In fact she had once found a lost Fox cub and nursed it and raised it with her own puppies. Let's see, that cub would be Foxy's uncle, or was it his father? He couldn't remember, it seemed so long ago.

Then evil days had fallen upon the Hill. The good Folks had moved away and their successors had been mean, shiftless, inconsiderate. Sumac, bayberry, and poison ivy had taken over the fields, the lawns had gone to crab grass and weeds, and there was no garden. Last autumn even

[14]

they had gone, leaving the empty house with its desolate black windows and its shutters flapping through the winter storms.

He passed the tool-house where in the old days bags of seed and chicken feed had always rewarded the hungry field mice. It had been empty for years; every grain of food had been searched out during the cold, hard winters. None of the Animals ever went there any more.

Porkey the Woodchuck was on the side lawn, hungrily snatching at the straggly patches of grass. His fur looked moth-eaten and he was quite thin — a very different animal from the fat, waddling Porkey who last fall had squeezed himself down his burrow to sleep away the winter. Now he was trying to make up for lost time. After each mouthful he would raise his head, look all around and grumble, then snatch another mouthful. It made his grumbling come in short bursts. "Look at this lawn," he growled, "just *look* at it — gulp-gulp — not a leaf of clover in it, nothing but crab grass and chickweed — gulp-gulp — *time* new Folks was coming — gulp-gulp — *high* time —" He paused and sat up as Father courteously greeted him.

"Good evening, Porkey, *good* evening. It is indeed a pleasure to see you about again. I trust you passed a mouthful of verbena to top off with—" He suddenly went back to his frantic tearing at the sparse grass patches.

Father continued his stroll in a happier frame of mind. After all, times *had* been pretty hard these last few years. Many of their friends had deserted the Hill; all their married children had sought other homes; Mother really was looking peaked and seemed to worry more and more. New Folks in the house might bring back the good old days—

"Good evening, sir, and good luck to you," said the Gray Fox politely. "New Folks coming, I understand."

"A pleasant good evening to *you*, sir," answered Father. "All indications seem to point to that happy event."

"I must thank you," the Fox went on, "for taking those Dogs off my trail yesterday morning. I wasn't in very good condition to deal with them. You see, I had been away up Weston way to bring home a hen—pickings are pretty scarce hereabouts these days. Eight miles it is, there and back, and she was a tough old girl. She was sitting pretty heavy and I was tuckered out when those Dogs jumped me. You handled them very skillful, very, and I am obliged to you."

"Not at all, my boy, not at all. Pray don't mention it," said Father. "I always enjoy a run to hounds. Brought up

on it, you know. Why down in the Bluegrass Country—"

"Yes, I know," said the Fox hastily. "What did you do with them?"

"Oh, just took them on a little romp down the Valley, through a few briar patches, ended them up on that electric fence of Jim Coley's. Stupid brutes, though. Hardly could call it sport, very low class. Now down in the Bluegrass Country the hounds were real thoroughbreds. Why, I can remember—"

"Yes, I know," said the Fox, melting into the bushes. "Thanks just the same, though."

[19]

The Gray Squirrel was digging around rather hopelessly. He never could quite remember where he'd buried his nuts, and there had been very few to bury last autumn anyway.

"Good evening, sir, and good luck to you," said Father. "The good luck, however, seems to be what you most require." He smiled as he eyed the futile diggings. "Your memory, old fellow, if you'll forgive my saying so, is not what it used to be."

"It never was," sighed the Squirrel. "Never *could* recollect where I put things." He paused to rest and looked out over the valley. "I can recollect other things, though, real clear. Do you remember the old days when things were good here on the Hill, when there was good Folks here? Mind the tree the young ones always used to fix for us, come Christmas? That spruce over there it was, only smaller then. Little lights onto it, carrots and cabbage leaves and celery for your folks, seed and suet for the birds (used to dip into them a bit myself), nuts, all kinds of nuts for us — and all hung pretty-like on the branches?"

"Indeed I do," said Father. "The memory of those times is deeply cherished by all of us, I am sure. Let us hope that the anticipated arrival of new Folks may, in some degree, bring about a renaissance of the old and pleasanter days."

"New Folks coming?" inquired the Squirrel quickly.

"It is so rumored, and recent developments seem to indicate such a possibility."

"Good," said the Squirrel, resuming his explorations with more energy. "Hadn't heard of it — been too busy scrabbling around. I've got the *most* forgetful memory — "

Willie Fieldmouse galloped along to the end of the mole ridge and whistled shrilly. "Mole," he shouted, "Mole, come up. News, Mole, news!"

Mole heaved head and shoulders up out of the earth and turned his blind face toward Willie, pointed snout quivering. "Well, Willie, well," he said, "what's all the excitement? What news is news?"

"News enough," Willie cried breathlessly. "Oh, Mole, *what* news! Everybody's talking about it. New Folks coming, Mole, NEW FOLKS COMING! In the Big House, new Folks. . . . Everybody says they're planting Folks, Mole, and maybe there'll be seeds again in the tool-house, seeds and chicken feed. And it'll fall through the cracks and we'll have all we can eat all winter, just like in summer. And there'll be heat in the cellar and we can build burrows right against the walls and be warm and snug again. And maybe they'll plant tulips, Mole, and scillas and chionodoxas. Oh, what wouldn't I give for a nice crisp tulip bulb right now!"

"Oh, that old bulb game." The Mole chuckled. "I know. I do all the digging and you follow up the burrow and eat the bulbs. That's fine for you, but what do I get out of it? Nothing but the blame, that's all *I* get."

"Why, Mole," said Willie, very hurt. "Why, Mole, that's unfair of you, it really is. You know what pals we've always been, always share and share alike. Why, Mole, I'm sur-prised—" He was snuffling slightly.

The Mole laughed and clapped Willie on the back with his broad, leathery paw. "Come, come"—he laughed—"don't be so everlastingly sensitive. I was only joking. Why, how could I get along without you, how could I know what was going on? How could I *see* things? What do I say when I want to see anything?"

Willie wiped away his snuffles. "You say, 'Willie, be eyes for me.'"

"Of course I do," said the Mole heartily. "I say, 'Willie, be eyes for me,' and you *are* eyes for me. You tell me just

how things look and the size of 'em and the colors of 'em. You tell it real good too. Nobody could tell it better."

Willie had lost his hurt now. "And I *do* tell you when mole traps have been set, don't I, or poison put out, and when they're going to roll the lawn, though nobody's rolled *this* lawn in a long time?"

"Of course you do." The Mole laughed. "Of course you do. Now blow your nose and run along. I've got my dinner to get, and grubs are scarce around here nowadays." He ducked back into his run, and Willie watched the ridge lengthen slowly down the lawn, the end of it heaving and quivering with the Mole's digging. He scampered down and rapped on the ground. "Mole," he cried, "I'll be eyes for you when *they* come. I'll tell you real good."

"Of course you will." Mole's voice was muffled by the earth. "Of course you will — and I wouldn't be surprised if there *was* tulips."

Phewie the Skunk stood up by the edge of the pine wood, looking down at the Big House. There was a slight rustle and the Red Buck appeared beside him. "Good evening, sir, and good luck to you," said Phewie. "New Folks coming."

"So I understand," said the Deer. "So I understand, and high time too, not that it matters to me especially. I roam a lot. But things have been poorly here on the Hill for some of the little fellows, very poorly."

"Yes, you roam," Phewie answered, "but you're not above a mess of garden sass now and then, are you?"

"Well, no, not if it's right to hand," the Buck admitted. He sniffed slightly. "I say, Phewie, you wouldn't mind moving over a bit, would you, a little to the leeward? There, that's fine. Thanks lots. As I was saying, I'm fairly fond of a mess of greens now and then, a row of lettuce, say, or some

young cabbage, very young—the old ones give me indiges-
tion—but of course what I really crave is tomatoes—*are*
tomatoes. You take a nice young ripe tomato, now—"

"You take it," interrupted Phewie. "Personally myself I
don't care whether they're planting Folks or not, except
for the rest of you, of course. Gardens are nothing in *my*
life. What *I'm* looking forward to is their garbidge."

"You do have such low tastes, Phewie," said the Buck.
"Er—by the way, the breeze seems to have shifted—would
you mind? There, that's fine, thanks. As I was saying—"

"Low taste nothing," answered Phewie indignantly. "You
just don't understand garbidge. Now there's garbidge *and*
garbidge, just like there's Folks and Folks. Some Folks'
garbidge just ain't fit for—well, it ain't even fitten for garbidge. But there's other garbidge, now, you couldn't ask for
anything nicer."

"*I* could," said the Deer firmly, "much nicer. By the way,
just to change the subject, Foxy's rather counting on there
being chickens, perhaps ducks, even. That ought to interest
you."

"Chickens is all right—young ones," admitted Phewie,
"and ducks is all right. But to get back to garbidge—"

"Oh dear," the buck groaned, "the wind's changed
again." And he backed into the woods.

[25]

Deep down in the cold ground, where some frost still lingered, the old Grandfather of all the Cutworms uncoiled his dirty gray length and stretched his stiff joints. His voice was a hissing whisper, but it served to waken from their winter sleep all the thousands of his offspring.

"New Folks coming," he hissed. "New Folks coming." Through all the sluggish mass the sound spread. Slowly a quiver ran through their ugly forms, slowly they uncoiled and began the long climb up through the clammy earth to be ready at the surface when the tender new plants should appear.

So it went on all over the Hill. Through the bushes and the tall, unkempt grass there was a continual stirring and rustling as the Little Animals rushed about, gossiping and speculating on the great event. The Squirrels and Chipmunks skittered along the stone walls, barking out the news. In the dark Pine Wood the Owl, the Crow, and the Bluejays argued over it loudly. Down in the burrows there was a ceaseless coming and going of visitors and above it all the ever recurring phrase, NEW FOLKS COMING.

2. Mother Worries

Down in the Rabbit burrow Mother was worrying harder than usual. Any occurrence, good or bad, which upset the quiet order of Mother's days always brought on a fit of worry, and of course the present great excitement had resulted in a perfect frenzy. She had thought of every danger or unpleasantness which might accompany the arrival of new Folks and was now inventing new and unlikely ones. She had discussed the possibility of Dogs, Cats, and Ferrets; of shotguns, rifles, and explosives; of traps and snares; of poisons and poison gases. There might even be *Boys!*

She had repeated a horrid rumor which had circulated recently, concerning a man who had attached a hose to the exhaust pipe of his automobile and stuck it down folks' burrows. Several families were reported to have perished from this diabolical practice.

"Now, Mother, now," Father had reassured her, "I have pointed out many times that their untimely fate was entirely due to their own negligence in allowing their emergency exits to become clogged with stored up foodstuffs. While a careful husbanding of food against the winter is a highly commendable custom, it is the height of folly to use one's emergency exit as a root cellar or a preserve closet.

"Unfortunately, or perhaps fortunately," he went on, eying their own bare shelves and empty cupboards, "our somewhat straitened circumstances of recent years have not permitted the accumulation of any great store of winter provender, so our exit has remained clear and in excellent repair at all times, although I must confess that you have occasionally exhibited an unfortunate tendency to clutter the passage with brooms, mops, buckets, and such unnecessary household implements. Just recently I experienced an extremely painful fall out there."

Mother had promptly removed the buckets and brooms and was somewhat comforted, but she still turned pale whenever the east wind brought a whiff of exhaust smell from some passing car.

She had also thought up the possibility that the newcomers might cut down and plow up the thicket where the burrow lay. This, Father admitted, was possible, but hardly probable. "In such an event," he said, "we should merely be forced to change our place of residence. Our present location down here in the hollow, although made dear through long association, is, at certain seasons of the year, indubitably damp, not to say wet. I have noted of late a slight tendency toward gout (a family inheritance) which might be greatly benefited by a removal to a somewhat more elevated location. I have long had my eye on a site up near the Pine Wood and, should such destructive activities on the part of new Folks necessitate a change of residence, it would, I believe, be not without certain advantages."

Mother burst into tears at the thought of leaving the old home, and Father hastily changed the subject to the possibility of Cats and Dogs.

"As for Cats," he said, "the whole matter is merely one of proper parental discipline. As you are aware, children should be heard but not seen. If they are kept indoors until large enough to properly take care of themselves, if they are taught to be always observant and alert, the danger from Cats is practically negligible. The Cat's capacity for sustained speed is laughable, her only weapon is surprise, and, if I may be pardoned for saying so, I believe I have been successful in teaching all *our* children to avoid ever being surprised.

"A few of the grandchildren, I regret to say, have been unduly pampered and allowed freedoms which were unknown in my day. The results of such parental indulgence have been swift and usually fatal. I hope, my son," he said, sternly glancing at Little Georgie, "I hope the lesson to be learned from the untimely feline ends of our grandchildren Minnie and Arthur, Wilfred, Sarah, Constance, Sarepta, Hogarth, and Clarence will not be lightly passed over by you."

Little Georgie promised that it would not. The mention of the little lost ones started Mother crying again, so Father continued. (He always continued until something stopped him.)

"Insofar as I am concerned, Dogs might well prove a very welcome addition to our community. Those country louts belonging to the Fat-Man-at-the-Crossroads are scarcely worthy of a gentleman's attention. I would really relish an occasional chase with a couple of highly bred hounds. Why down in the Bluegrass Country where I was reared—"

"Yes, I know," Mother broke in, "I know about the Bluegrass Country, but there's Porkey. He's one of your closest friends—"

"Porkey *is* a problem," Father admitted. "His foolish choice of a home site right up there in the very shadow of the Big House was most unwise, as I have often pointed

out to him. Of course with the former tenants it didn't matter. He could have lived in their parlor for all they cared. But with the advent of Dogs, his present location would be dangerous in the extreme. Should the personnel of the incoming menage include Dogs, I shall have to take up the matter with him again and be very firm."

But Mother was having a good worry and refused to be distracted. "There's the spring housecleaning," she fretted. "I'd been planning to get at *that* this week, but what with all the goings on, folks running in and out, there just doesn't seem to be a chance. And there's Uncle Analdas, him living way up Danbury way and Mildred married and left him all alone and him getting old and what a state his burrow is in by now I can't imagine. I'd been counting on asking him down for the summer, spite of the food shortage. But now with new Folks coming and Dogs maybe and traps and snares and spring-guns or maybe poison, I just don't know— I just don't know—"

"As a matter of fact," said Father, "I can think of no more propitious a time for your Uncle Analdas' visit, for several reasons. Item one: he is, as you point out, extremely lonely since Mildred's departure, hence a change of surroundings will doubtless prove highly beneficial. Item two: the food situation up Danbury way is, I understand, even more acute than ours; therefore if our new Folks turn out to be plant-ing people, as we have every reason to expect, his situation in respect to edibles will be vastly improved. In short, he will eat good. Item three: Uncle Analdas, being the oldest member of the family now extant, has had many years of experience with man and his ways. Should our newcomers prove to be difficult people, which I do not anticipate, but it is always well to consider every eventuality, his advice and counsel will prove invaluable in dealing with such problems as might arise.

"Therefore I should advise sending for Uncle Analdas at once. I would be delighted to go myself were it not for the great number of pressing matters which will demand my attention here during the next few days. This being true, the duty must fall to Little Georgie."

Little Georgie's heart leaped with excitement at the prospect, but he managed to lie quietly while Mother did a fresh bit of worrying and Father allayed her fears — as much as possible. After all, he *was* a pretty big boy now, he could run almost as fast as Father, and he knew most of the tricks. For the past few months he had done all the marketing at the Fat-Man's-at-the-Crossroads, had easily avoided the Dogs, and crossed the Black Road safely twice each day. He knew the way to Uncle Analdas' — they had all gone up for Mildred's wedding last fall. Why shouldn't he go? Of course he hated to miss a moment on the Hill with all that was going on, but a trip clear up Danbury way *was* exciting, and he would only be gone two days. Nothing much could happen in that time.

As he drifted off to sleep he could hear Mother still worrying and Father talking on and on — and on — and — on —

3. Little Georgie Sings a Song

IT was barely daylight when Little Georgie started his
journey. In spite of her worrying, Mother had managed to put up a small but nourishing lunch. This, along
with a letter to Uncle Analdas, was packed in a little

knapsack and slung over his shoulder. Father went along as far as the Twin Bridges. As they stepped briskly down the Hill the whole valley was a lake of mist on which rounded treetops swam like floating islands. From old orchards rose a mounting chorus as the birds greeted the new day. Mothers chirped and chuckled and scolded as they swept and tidied the nests. On the topmost branches their menfolk warbled and shrilled and mocked one another.

The houses were all asleep, even the Dogs of the Fat-Man-at-the-Crossroads were quiet, but the Little Animals were up and about. They met the Gray Fox returning from a night up Weston way. He looked footsore and sleepy, and a few chicken feathers still clung to his ruff. The Red Buck trotted daintily across the Black Road to wish them good luck and good morning, but Father, for once, had no time for long social conversation. This was business, and no Rabbit in the county knew his business any better than Father— few as well.

"Now, son," he said firmly, "your mother is in a very nervous state and you are not to add to her worries by taking unnecessary risks or by carelessness. No dawdling and no foolishness. Keep close to the road but well off it. Watch your bridges and your crossings. What do you do when you come to a bridge?"

"I hide well," answered Georgie, "and wait a good long time. I look all around for Dogs. I look up the road for cars and down the road for cars. When everything's clear I run across — fast. I hide again and look around to be sure I've not been seen. Then I go on. The same thing for crossings."

"Good," said Father. "Now recite your Dogs."

Little Georgie closed his eyes and dutifully recited, "Fat-Man-at-the-Crossroads: two Mongrels; Good Hill Road: Dalmatian; house on Long Hill: Collie, noisy, no wind; Norfield Church corner: Police Dog, stupid, no nose; On the High Ridge, red farmhouse: Bulldog and Setter, both fat, don't bother; farmhouse with the big barns: Old Hound, very dangerous..." and so on. He recited every dog on the route clear up to Danbury way. He did it without a mistake and swelled with pride at Father's approving nod.

"Excellent," said Father. "Now do you remember your checks and doublings?" Little Georgie closed his eyes again and rattled off, quite fast, "Sharp right and double left, double left and double right, dead stop and back flip, right jump, left jump, false trip, and briar dive."

"Splendid," said Father. "Now attend carefully. Size up your Dog; don't waste speed on a plodder, you may need it later. If he's a rusher, check, double, and freeze. Your freeze, by the way, is still rather bad. You have a tendency to flick

[37]

your left ear; you must watch that. The High Ridge is very open country so keep in the shadow of the stone walls and mark the earth piles. Porkey has lots of relatives along there, and if you are pressed hard any of them will gladly take you in. Just tell them who you are, and don't forget to thank them. After a chase, hide up and take at least ten minutes' rest. And if you have to *really* run, tighten that knapsack strap, lace back your ears, put your stomach to the ground, and RUN!

"Get along with you now, and mind — no foolishness. We shall expect you and Uncle Analdas by tomorrow evening at the latest."

Little Georgie crossed the Twin Bridges in perfect form, returned Father's approving wave, and was off on his own.

It was gray and misty as he crossed Good Hill Road, and the Dalmatian still slept. So, apparently, did the Collie up the road, for all was quiet as he plodded up Long Hill. People were beginning to stir as he approached Norfield Church corner; little plumes of blue smoke were rising from kitchen chimneys, and the air was pleasant with the smell of frying bacon.

As he expected, the Police Dog rushed him there, but he wasted little time on that affair. Loping along with tantalizing slowness until they were almost on an old fallen

apple tree buried in briars, he executed a dead stop, a right jump, and a freeze. The bellowing brute over-ran him and plunged headlong into the thorny tangle. His agonized howls were sweet music to Little Georgie as he hopped sedately along toward the High Ridge. He wished Father had been there to see how skillfully he had worked and to note that during the freeze his left ear hadn't flickered once.

The sun was well up when he emerged on the High Ridge. On the porch of the red farmhouse the fat Bulldog and the Setter slept soundly, soaking up its warmth. On any other occasion Little Georgie would have been tempted to wake them to enjoy their silly efforts at running, but, mindful of Father's instructions, he kept dutifully on his way.

The High Ridge was a long and open strip of country, very uninteresting to Little Georgie. The view, over miles and miles of rolling woods and meadows, was very beautiful, but he didn't care especially about views. The brilliant blue sky and the bright little cream-puff clouds were beautiful too. They made him feel good; so did the warm sun, but frankly he was becoming slightly bored. So to ease his boredom he began to make a little song.

The words had been rattling around in his head for some days now, and the music was there too, but he couldn't quite get them straight and fitted together. So he hummed and he sang and he whistled. He tried the words this way and that way, he stopped and started and changed the notes around, and finally he got the first line so that it suited him. So Georgie sang that line over and over again to be sure that he wouldn't forget it when he started on the second line.

It must have been this preoccupation with his song that made Little Georgie careless and almost led to his undoing. He scarcely noticed that he had passed the house with the big barns, and he was just starting to sing his first line for the forty-seventh time when there came the roaring rush of the Old Hound right on his heels, so close that he could feel the hot breath.

Instinctively Little Georgie made several wild springs that carried him temporarily out of harm's way. He paused a fraction of a second to tighten the knapsack strap and then set off at a good steady pace. "Don't waste speed on a plodder" was Father's rule. He tried a few checks and doubles and circlings, although he knew they were pretty useless. The great fields were too bare, and the Old Hound knew all the tricks. No matter how he turned and dodged, the Hound was always there, coming along at his heavy gallop. He looked for Woodchuck burrows, but there were none in sight. "Well, I guess I'll have to run it out," said Little Georgie.

He pulled the knapsack strap tighter, laced back his ears, put his stomach to the ground, and RAN. And *how* he ran!

The warm sun had loosened his muscles; the air was invigorating; Little Georgie's leaps grew longer and longer. Never had he felt so young and strong. His legs were like coiled springs of steel that released themselves of their own accord. He was hardly conscious of any effort, only of his hind feet pounding the ground, and each time they hit, those wonderful springs released and shot him through the air. He sailed over fences and stone walls as though they were mole runs. Why, this was almost like flying! Now he understood what Zip the Swallow had been driving at when

he tried to describe what it was like. He glanced back at the Old Hound, far behind now, but still coming along at his plodding gallop. He was old and must be tiring, while he, Little Georgie, felt stronger and more vigorous at every leap. Why didn't the old fool give up and go home?

And then, as he shot over the brow of a slight rise, he suddenly knew. *He had forgotten Deadman's Brook!* There it lay before him, broad and deep, curving out in a great silvery loop. He, the son of Father, gentleman hunter from the Bluegrass, had been driven into a trap, a trap that even Porkey should have been able to avoid! Whether he turned to right or left the loop of the creek hemmed him in and the Old Hound could easily cut him off. There was nothing for it but to jump!

This sickening realization had not reduced his speed;
now he redoubled it. The slope helped, and his soaring
leaps became prodigious. The wind whistled through his
laced-back ears. Still he kept his head, as Father would
have wished him to. He picked a spot where the bank was
high and firm; he spaced his jumps so they would come out
exactly right.

The take-off was perfect. He put every ounce of leg
muscle into that final kick and sailed out into space. Below
him he could see the cream-puff clouds mirrored in the

dark water, he could see the pebbles on the bottom and the silver flash of frightened minnows dashing away from his flying shadow. Then, with a breath-taking thump, he landed, turned seven somersaults, and came up sitting in a clump of soft lush grass.

He froze, motionless except for heaving sides, and watched the Old Hound come thundering down the slope, slide to a stop and, after eying the water disgustedly, take his way slowly homeward, his dripping tongue almost dragging the ground.

Little Georgie did not need to remember Father's rule for a ten-minute rest after a good run. He was blown and he knew it, but he did remember his lunch, so he unstrapped the little knapsack and combined lunch and rest. He had been really scared for a moment, but as his wind came back and his lunch went down, his spirits came up.

Father would be angry, and rightly, for he had made two very stupid mistakes: he had let himself be surprised, and he had run right into a dangerous trap. But that leap! Never in the history of the county had any rabbit jumped Deadman's Brook, not even Father. He marked the exact spot and calculated the width of the stream there — at least eighteen feet! And with his rising spirits the words and the notes of his song suddenly tumbled into place.

New Folks co-ming, Oh my! New Folks co-ming, Oh my! New Folks co-ming, Oh my! Oh my! Oh my!

Little Georgie lay back in the warm grass and sang his
song —

New Folks coming, oh my!
New Folks coming, oh my!
New Folks coming, oh my!
Oh my! Oh my!

There weren't many words and there weren't many notes,
and the notes just went up a little and down a little and
ended where they began. Lots of people might have

[45]

thought it monotonous, but it suited Little Georgie completely. He sang it loud and he sang it soft, he sang it as a paean of triumph, a saga of perils met and overcome. He sang it over and over again.

Red-bellied Robin, flying northward, paused in a sapling and called down, "Hi, Little Georgie, what're you doing way up here?"

"Going to fetch Uncle Analdas. Have you been by the Hill?"

"Just left there," Robin answered. "Everybody's excited. Seems there's new Folks coming."

"Yes, I know," cried Little Georgie eagerly. "I've just made a song about it. Wouldn't you like to hear it? It goes like —"

"No, thanks," called Robin. "Getting along —" And he flew on.

Not in the least discouraged, Little Georgie sang his song a few times more while he strapped on his knapsack and took up his journey. It was a good song to walk to, too, so he sang it as he tramped the rest of the High Ridge, as he went down the Windy Hill and circled around George-town. He was still singing it in the late afternoon when he got clear up Danbury way.

He had just finished "Oh my!" for the four-thousandth

time when a sharp voice from the bushes broke in with, "Oh my — *what?*"

Little Georgie whirled. "Oh my — *goodness!*" he cried. "Why — why it's Uncle Analdas."

"Sure is." The voice chuckled. "Uncle Analdas as ever was. Come in, Little Georgie, come in — you're a long way from home. Ef I'd been a Dog I'd got you. Surprised yer Old Man ain't learned you more care. Come in anyhow."

Although Mother had worried about the state of Uncle Analdas' home with no feminine hands around to keep things neat, she could never, in her most pessimistic moments, have pictured anything quite so disorderly as the burrow to which Little Georgie was welcomed.

It was a man's home, there could be no doubt about that, and while Little Georgie rather admired the bachelor freedom of the place, he was forced to admit that it really was extremely dirty and the fleas numerous and active. After his day in the open air the atmosphere indoors seemed stifling and not at all fragrant. Perhaps it was the sort of tobacco that Uncle Analdas smoked — Little Georgie hoped so. His Uncle's cooking too left something to be desired — their supper consisted of one very ancient and dried-up turnip. After this meager meal they sat outside, at Little Georgie's suggestion, and Mother's letter was produced.

"S'pose you read it to me, Georgie," said Uncle Analdas. "Seem to've mislaid them dingblasted spectacles." Little Georgie knew that he hadn't mislaid them, in fact that he didn't own any; he'd just never learned to read, but this formality always had to be gone through with, so he dutifully read:

Dear Uncle Analdas:

I hope this finds you well but I know you are lonesome with Mildred married and gone away and all and we are hoping you will spend the summer with us as we have new Folks coming and we hope they are planting Folks and if they are we will all eat good but they may have Dogs or poison or traps and spring-guns and maybe you shouldn't risk your life although you haven't much of it left but we will be looking forward to seeing you anyway.

Your loving niece,
Mollie.

There was a postscript which said, "P.S. Please don't let Little Georgie get his feet wet," but Georgie didn't read that out loud. The idea! He, Little Georgie, who had jumped Deadman's Brook, Little Georgie the Leaper, getting his feet wet!

"Well now," cried Uncle Analdas. "Well now, that's a real nice letter, real nice. Don't know but what I will. Certainly is dingblasted lonesome 'round here now, with Millie gone and all. And as for food—of all the carrot-pinchin', stingy folks I ever see, the Folks around here is the stingiest, carrot-pinchin'est. Yes sir, I think I will. Course new Folks comin' may be good and it may be bad. Either way I don't trust 'em. Don't trust old Folks neither. But with old Folks you kin tell just how much you *can't* trust 'em, and with new Folks you can't tell *nothing*. Think I'll do it, though, think I will. Does yer maw still make that peavine and lettuce soup as good as she used to?"

Little Georgie assured him that she still did and wished he had a bowl of it right then. "I've made up a song about the new Folks," he added eagerly. "Would you like to hear it?"

"Don't think I would," answered Uncle Analdas. "Sleep anywheres you've a mind to, Georgie. I've got a few knick-knacks to pack up, and we'd ought to get an early start. I'll wake you."

Little Georgie decided to sleep outside under the bushes. The evening was quite warm and the burrow was really pretty strong. He hummed his song, as a lullaby now, and it was a good lullaby, for before he'd finished it the third time he was sound asleep.

4. Uncle Analdas

T HEY started early, for Uncle Analdas really was getting quite elderly and had to travel at a leisurely pace.
What he lacked in speed, however, was more than made
up for by his craft and intimate knowledge of the country-
side. He knew every path and short cut, every Dog and
every hiding place. All day he instructed Little Georgie in

the tricks of the Rabbit trade, about which he knew almost more than Father.

They kept to the shadow of the stone walls and hedgerows; they circled wide around every house that possessed dangerous Dogs; when they paused for rest it was always within one leap of a burrow or briar patch. They stopped for lunch at Deadman's Brook, and Little Georgie, with pardonable pride, pointed out the exact spot where he had jumped it. They even found the deep footprints that marked his landing.

Uncle Analdas eyed the broad stream with a shrewd and practiced eye. "Quite a leap, Georgie," he admitted. "*Quite* a leap. Yer Old Man couldn't do it, couldn't a done it myself, not even in my prime. Yes *sir*—quite a leap. Shouldn't a let yourself get surprised though, shouldn't a let yourself get driven into no fix like that neither, no sir, that was plumb careless. Don't think your Old Man'll like *that*." Little Georgie was sure he would not.

The lunch was a very poor one indeed, for it consisted of the scrapings of Uncle Analdas' larder, never too bountiful at best. But the sun was warm, the sky was blue, and the old gentleman seemed inclined to rest and discourse.

"D'you know, Georgie," he said, settling back comfortably in the deep grass, "that there song you've been a-singin' at all day—it ain't much of a song and it ain't much of a tune, but there's real good *sense* to it, though you probably don't know it. And I'll tell you why—because there always *is* new Folks comin', that's why. There's always new Folks comin' and always new times comin'.

"Why, look at this here very road we're a-travelin' along. I mind my grandfather tellin' me how his grandfather told *him* how *his* grandfather used to tell about the old, old days and how the British red-coat soldiers come a-trampin' up this road, clear up Danbury way, a-roarin' and a-shootin' and a-burnin' of the houses and the barns and the crops, an' how the folks hereabouts come a-rampagin' and a-shootin' of them. And a lot of them was buried right in these here orchards and all the homes was gone and all the critters and the food was gone and they was Bad Times then—real bad. But them soldiers went away and them times went away and there was always new Folks comin' and new times comin'.

"Us folks just went on a-raisin' of our young ones and a-tendin' to our own affairs, but new Folks kept a-comin' and after a while this here whole valley was full of little mills and factories and all them fields there along the High Ridge was growin' thick with wheat and potatoes and onions and Folks was everywhere and the big wagons

[53]

a-rumblin' and a-rollin' along this very road, just a-spillin' out grain and hay and all. Them was Good Times, for everybody.

"But then pretty soon all the young men Folks went a-marchin' down this here road, all of 'em wearin' blue uniforms, a-singin' an' a-laughin' an' carryin' paper sacks of cookies an' flowers stuck into their guns. Most of them never come back, an' the old Folks petered out or went away an' the mills fell in an' the fields growed up in weeds an' then it was Bad Times again. But Grandad and Gran-mammy just went on a-raisin' us and tendin' their own business an' then there was new Folks comin' *again*, an' black roads an' new houses an' schools an' automobiles an' first thing you know it was Good Times again.

"There's Good Times, Georgie, an' there's Bad Times, but they go. An' there's good Folks an' there's bad Folks, an' they go too—but there's always new Folks comin'. That's why there's some sense in that song you keep a-singin'—though it's real tedious otherwise, real tedious. I'm goin' to take a nap—ten minutes. Keep your eyes open."

Little Georgie kept his eyes open and his ears cocked; he wasn't going to be surprised again. He started to think about the things that Uncle Analdas had told him, but thinking always made him sleepy, so he washed his face and paws in the stream, packed up their knapsacks, and watched the shadow of a twig on the bank. When it showed that a full ten minutes had elapsed he woke his uncle and they continued on their way.

Word of Uncle Analdas' departure had spread among the Little Animals up Danbury way and many of them came out along the roadside to wish him good-by and good luck. The Woodchucks too, along the High Ridge, all wanted to send messages to Porkey, so it was late afternoon when they tramped down Long Hill toward the Twin Bridges. They were tired and hot and dusty now, and as they approached the north branch Uncle Analdas seemed to have something weighty on his mind. While they rested on the bank of the stream he suddenly unburdened himself.

"Georgie," he burst forth, "I'm a-goin' to do it, yes *sir*, I'm a-goin' to do it. You know, women folks is funny like and particular about some things and your maw is *extra* particular. I dunno how many dingblasted years it is since I've done it, but I'm a-goin' to do it now."

"Do what?" asked Little Georgie, puzzled.

"Georgie," said Uncle Analdas solemnly, "listen careful now, because you may never hear me speak these words again in your whole life. Georgie—*I'm goin' to take me a bath!*"

Clean, refreshed, and slicked up, they hastened toward the Hill, Little Georgie almost running in his eagerness to be home. Even from a distance it was clear that things had happened in his absence, for on the roof of the Big House shone patches of bright new shingles, and the air was fragrant with the smell of pine shavings and fresh paint.

They were greeted joyfully by Mother and Father, and while Uncle Analdas settled his few knickknacks in the guest room Little Georgie burst into an account of his adventures. Father, of course, was quite angry at his carelessness in allowing the Old Hound to surprise him, but became so swollen with pride over the great leap across Deadman's Brook that he was less severe than he might have been.

"And, Mother," Little Georgie went on excitedly, "I've made a song. It goes —"

Father raised his paw for silence. "Listen," he said. They listened, and at first Little Georgie heard nothing; then suddenly the sound came to him.

All over the Hill the voices of the Little Animals were rising in a chorus, and they were singing *his* song—the Song of Little Georgie!

Way up near the house he could hear Porkey's unmusical bellow, "*New Folks comin', Oh my!*" He could recognize the voices of Phewie, of the Red Buck and the Gray Fox. The piping treble of Willie Fieldmouse and all his brothers and sisters rose like a tiny, faraway chime. *"Oh my, Oh my!"* He could hear the Mole's muffled voice coming up from the sod. Mother hummed it as she bustled about, preparing dinner. Even Uncle Analdas, sniffing happily at the soup pot, chimed in with an occasional cracked, *"Oh my!"*

Bill Hickey and his carpenters were just leaving, and as their truck rattled down the drive Little Georgie could hear them all whistling—whistling *his* tune!

At the cottage down the road Tim McGrath hammered happily at his tractor, getting it in shape after the long winter's idleness. His plow was all cleaned and polished, his harrow lay ready. And as he worked he sang a song.

"Where did you get that song?" asked his wife Mary from the kitchen window.

"Don't know," said Tim. *"Oh my! New Folks comin', oh my! New Folks—"*

"And it's a good thing," interrupted Mary. "It's a good thing new folks are coming, after the winter we've had and not much work and all. It's a good thing."

"—comin', oh my! Plenty of work now," he cried. "Garden to be made, big garden; lawns done over, North Field plowed and seeded, wood cut, brush cleared, drive fixed, shrubs moved, chicken run, lots of work—*Oh my, oh my! New Folks comin', oh—"*

"I don't think that's much of a song," said Mary, "but it's a Good Thing."

Nevertheless, a few minutes later, above the rattle of the supper dishes Tim could hear her not unmusical voice crooning contentedly, *"—coming, oh my! New Folks coming, oh my!"*

Louie Kernstawk, the mason, was loading his truck. As

he threw in trowels and buckets and hammers, shovels, hose, cement bags, and all the other things he would need tomorrow, he hummed, much off tune but very happily. It would have been hard to tell what the notes were, and the words were indistinct too, but it sounded like "—*Folks coming, oh my! New Folks coming*—"

Down at the Corner Store, Mr. Daley was arranging his shelves and ordering new stock. He didn't need to order much, for it had been a long, hard winter; few people had been about, and his shelves were almost as full as they had been last fall. But now winter was over; through the open door the first warm air of spring crept softly in; from the swamp the peeper-frogs clamored like jangling sleigh bells.

Mr. Daley sat on his high stool and scratched at his lists, and as he wrote he sang a little song—"*New Folks*—coffee two dozen, corned beef, twelve—*coming, oh my! New Folks*—starch three cartons, matches, pepper, cornstarch, salt, gingerale—*coming, oh my! New Folks coming*—paper napkins, vinegar, dill pickles, dried apricots—*oh my!*

"*Oh my! Oh my!*"

5. Porkey Sits Tight

THE NEXT few days saw great doings on the Hill. In fact there was so much going on that Father was fairly worn out, keeping an eye on things. The vegetable garden was plowed, harrowed, and raked. It was a good generous garden, double its former size, and to everyone's relief there was no fence around it. The flower beds had been cultivated and fertilized, all the lawns dug up, raked, and rolled, ready for reseeding.

Now the North Field was being plowed. Tim McGrath, riding his roaring tractor, whistled happily as he watched the brown earth roll from the plowshare in clean, straight furrows. From the door of Porkey's home Porkey and Father watched the proceedings approvingly. As the tractor ceased its roaring momentarily, Louie Kernstawk, rebuilding a stone wall, called to Tim, "What're they going to plant there, Tim?"

"Buckwheat," he replied. "Buckwheat now. Later turn it under and plant clover and timothy."

"Did you hear *that?*" Porkey nudged Father gleefully. "*Buckwheat!* Why, I ain't had myself into a good field of buckwheat in I don't know when. Oh my, oh my!"

"You haven't heard any mention of bluegrass, have you?" asked Father hopefully.

"No, I ain't," said Porkey. "But *I* can do with buckwheat, not having no fancy Kentucky stummick. Reckon your old lady will be glad to hear about this too. Them little buckwheat cakes she used to make was mighty fine. Jus' think!" He sighed ecstatically. "A whole field of buckwheat, and right in my front yard, as you might say."

[62]

"Mention of your front yard reminds me, Porkey," Father began, "that I must talk seriously with you concerning the dangers inherent in your present location. Should the newcomers—"

Porkey interrupted him rudely. "If all them words mean that you're starting in again to talk about my moving, you might as well save your wind. I ain't a-goin' to do it." He hunched his shoulders stubbornly. "*I just ain't a-goin' to do it*, and that's that. There ain't a finer burrow nowheres on this Hill. I've worked hard on this place and—I ain't a-goin' to do it."

"As I was saying," Father continued, "should the newcomers introduce Dogs to our midst, your situation here, immediately adjacent to the house, would be perilous in the extreme."

"Kin take care of myself," Porkey muttered.

"No one desires to cast reflections on your personal courage, Porkey, nor on your ability to fend for yourself," Father was becoming slightly impatient now, "but your stubborn and unreasonable attitude is causing your friends a great deal of pain.

"I have talked the matter over with the Buck and the Gray Fox, and we are firmly resolved that should there be Dogs and you still persist in your refusal to listen to reason, we shall, much as we might regret it, be reduced to the use of force to remove you bodily to a safer location. We have also talked it over with Phewie, who is in perfect agreement with us. He can, as you know, render your home unfit for habitation in a very few moments and is fully prepared to do so, should it become necessary."

Having delivered this ultimatum, Father stalked away, but Porkey merely humped his shoulders more stubbornly and continued to mutter, "Ain't a-goin' to do it. Ain't a-goin' to do it."

Father found Phewie and the Gray Fox inspecting the newly repaired chicken house and run. The run was built of stout wire but the Gray Fox had already chosen and marked the spot where he planned to tunnel under it. Phewie, who preferred the younger chicks, was contemplating digging under the coop itself. "A nice tender one now and then is fine," he was saying, "but I wouldn't be bothering with them if I was sure what the garbidge situation's going to be. What *I* hope is they ain't going to have one of them new-fangled garbidge cans that's buried in the ground, them ones with heavy iron lids. Why, they're downright dangerous, oughtn't to be allowed.

"Had a cousin over here to Charcoal Hill got caught in one of 'em. Got it open all right and was enjoying himself when *ker-bam*, down come the lid and there he was. In there all night. He sure had enough of garbidge, time the maid come out next morning. She got enough of Skunk, too, when she opened up that lid." He chuckled. "Left that day, she did. Served them Folks right, having any such dangerous contraption."

"Perhaps they will dig a pit and bury it," Father suggested.

"Don't hold with that neither," Phewie answered. "A plumb waste that is, mixing nice fresh garbidge with old stale garbidge and tin cans and dirt and all. No sir, what I like to see is a good old-fashioned garbidge can with a nice, loose-fitting lid, and if these Folks is thoughtful, considerate-acting Folks, that's the kind of can they'll have."

Father found the subject a bit distasteful so he continued his stroll and soon came across Willie Fieldmouse and his friend Mole.

"Good evening, William," said Father. "I trust that all your friends and relatives succeeded in removing their mousehold goods from the North Field before the plowing began?"

"Yes indeed, sir, thank you kindly," answered Willie politely. "And they are all very grateful to you for warning them in time."

"Not at all, not at all," replied Father. "I merely chanced to overhear Mr. McGrath remark that he was starting it next day and was thus enabled to spread the word. I only wish that certain other people were as quick to respond to suggestions made for their own good."

"You mean Porkey?" asked Willie. "Ain't he the stubborn old codger?"

Father regarded Willie severely. "*Mister* Porkey, William, is one of the very oldest and most highly regarded members of our community and as such he is entitled to a certain amount of respect from flippant young people."

"Yes *sir*," said Willie.

"Mole," Father went on, surveying the smoothly raked front lawn, "this is a very beautiful piece of grading. You should enjoy some splendid burrowing here."

The Mole picked up a bit of soil and crumbled it in his paw. "A little soft yet for good digging," he said, "and then all the grubs are scattered and scared away. But in two-three weeks now, when the young grass gets a good start and the grubs gather again (nothing they love like good tender grass roots, you know), then I'm going to have myself some *real* hunting."

At this moment Little Georgie galloped up, fairly bursting with news. "Coming tomorrow, Paw," he shouted. "Coming tomorrow. I just heard Louie Kernstawk telling Tim McGrath they ought to get those holes in the driveway filled up on account of the moving vans are coming tomorrow. The Folks too—coming tomorrow."

"Splendid," said Father. "At last we shall be enabled to ascertain the character and disposition of our new neighbors and learn what canine or feline hazards may accompany them. By the way, Georgie, do not mention moving vans in your Mother's presence. You remember Little Throckmorton?"

Little Georgie did, very well, for Throckmorton had been one of Mother's very favorite grandchildren. A moving van had been the cause of *his* taking off, and Mother had had an unreasoning terror of them ever since.

The news, of course, spread like wildfire; all that evening the burrow was filled with chatter and speculation and the coming and going of callers. Father's caution about the mention of vans was futile, for the moment Mother learned that the arrival of the new Folks was imminent she cried, "Moving vans," and burst into tears. She threw her apron over her head and wept for some time, demanding that Little Georgie be confined to the burrow on the morrow until all danger was past.

"Naow Mollie, don't take on so," consoled Uncle Analdas. "Ain't no sense to it. Why with that bumpity, twisty driveway full of holes like it is, couldn't no dingblasted movin' van make speed enough to danger a box turtle. Besides, *I'll* be there, and what I don't know about movin' vans, and Folks and Dogs *and* Cats, nobody don't know."

Mother vowed that she would not stir from the burrow the entire day, but Uncle Analdas poked Father in the ribs. "Don't worry." He chuckled. "She'll be out there, right along of all the rest of us, a-lookin' and a-watchin'. I know about women too."

[68]

6. Moving Vans

THE GREAT DAY dawned and the moving vans came.
They creaked, swayed, and rumbled up the driveway,
their drivers completely unaware that they were being
watched by dozens of pairs of small, bright eyes. In bayberry clumps, in thickets and long grass, all the Little Animals were gathered to inspect the new arrivals. The Gray
Fox and the Red Buck had come to the edge of the Pine

Wood, where they stood, motionless as statues, except when the Buck's great ears turned this way and that to gather in each errant sound. Even Mother had ventured forth, once the vans had come to rest, and now sat between Father and Uncle Analdas, keeping a firm grip on Little Georgie's left ear.

For the Animals there was a great interest in seeing the furniture unloaded for it afforded an opportunity to judge the character of the new Folks by their possessions. Father noted approvingly the rich sheen of many pieces of old mahogany. "Those," he whispered to Mother, "very clearly indicate quality Folks. I have not seen anything of that sort since I left the Bluegrass—"

He was interrupted by Phewie's joyful wiggling. A large old-fashioned garbage can without any lid at all had just been put out behind the garage. "Now that's what I call *real* Folks," Phewie gloated, "and right there under the grape arbor. I can have dinner *and* dessert right in the one place."

Uncle Analdas was watching with sharp eye the various tools and garden implements that were going into the tool-house. "Ain't seen no traps nor spring-guns yet," he admitted. "There's a lot of cans and jugs, though—may be poisons and they may not—can't tell yet."

Louie Kernstawk and Tim McGrath had both found occasion to putter around near the house so they too could
observe and judge. "Look like nice Folks' things," said
Louie.

"Yes," answered Tim, "real nice. There's an awful lot of
books, though. Don't hold much with that. People that
reads books much seem to be queer-like. Grandpa always
said, 'Readin' rots the mind.' Don't know but what he was
right."

"Oh, I don't know," Louie observed, "I knew a feller
once read books a lot and he was *real* nice. Died a couple
of years ago."

The moving vans discharged their loads and creaked
away down the drive, but the Animals never stirred. Their
concern really was the Folks. It was midafternoon before
their patience was finally rewarded by the sight of a car

coming up the drive. It was a fairly old car, bulging with baggage. A stir of excitement swept through the watching Animals, and every eye was fixed on the occupants.

The Man got out first. He was smoking a pipe, and Uncle Analdas sniffed the air approvingly. "Now *there's* something I like," he said quietly to Father. "I like a man as smokes a pipe. Gives you some warning. You take some of these fellers now, they'll come a-walkin' through a field when you're maybe takin' a nap, and almost step on your dingblasted back 'fore you know they're comin'. But you take a feller smokin' a pipe, specially a good strong one like that, why you'll know he's comin' half a mile away. Yes *sir*, I like pipes."

Father nodded agreement, but his eyes were fixed on the Lady. She had lifted a large basket from the car and was now opening the lid.

Mother caught her breath, and a shiver passed through all the little Fieldmice as an enormous tiger-striped gray Cat stepped forth. He stretched his front legs and he stretched his hind legs, then with slow and dignified pace stalked up to the front doorstep and began to take a bath. He bathed thoroughly, even spreading out his paws and licking well between the toes; then he settled down in the sunshine and went to sleep.

The Fieldmice were chattering and whispering their fright, Mother seemed about to faint, but Uncle Analdas, whose practiced eye had noted many things, soon stilled their fears. "Old," he pronounced. "Older than all get out. Didn't you notice how stiff-like he walked? And them teeth —didn't you see 'em when he yawned, nothin' but old rounded stumps? Shucks, he couldn't danger nobody. I'd just as soon walk up and kick him in the face—will, too, one of these days."

Their attention now returned to the car, which was quivering and creaking strangely. Two or three bundles fell out, then a whole shower of them, as a very stout colored woman heaved her vast bulk out of the rear door.

"Well, Sulphronia, here's our new home. Isn't it going to be lovely?" the Lady said brightly. Sulphronia looked rather doubtful and, lugging two bulging suitcases, waddled off toward the kitchen door.

Phewie slapped Father on the back gleefully. "Will there be garbidge? *Will* there? Oh my, oh my! I've never seen one that shape and color that didn't set out the elegantest garbidge! Lots of it too; chicken wings, duck's backs, hambones—and cooked to a turn!"

"They are, of course, splendid cooks," Father admitted, "and as a rule extremely generous and understanding of our

[73]

needs and customs. Very rare up here, but down in the Bluegrass Country where—"

"Oh, you and your bluegrass—" interrupted Phewie.

"Stow your gab and keep your eyes open," said Uncle Analdas sharply. "See if they unload any traps or spring-guns, poisons, rifles, shotguns, snares, nets, any of them things."

They watched until every last bag and bundle had been unloaded and taken within. They watched until the late-afternoon shadows spread over the Cat, saw him rise stiffly, stretch, and pace around to the kitchen door. Then they scattered to their separate homes, talking over the events of the day as they went.

On the whole everyone felt quite satisfied. There had been no sign of traps, spring-guns, or other lethal weapons; the Cat was obviously harmless; and there were no Dogs.

As night settled down it was pleasant to see lights in the Big House again, to see people stirring and hear the cheery clatter of dishes from the kitchen. The odor of hickory smoke was pleasant on the air. Little Georgie, passing close to the House, could hear a log fire crackling in the living room. Happily he hummed:

New Folks is come, oh my!
New Folks is come, oh my!

7. Reading Rots the Mind

ALTHOUGH the new Folks may not have realized it, they were very decidedly on probation for the next few days. All day small bright eyes in the long grass watched their every movement, small ears were cocked to hear their every word.

On the very first morning Father and Uncle Analdas decided to try out the Cat, whose name, they had learned, was

Mr. Muldoon. He was lying on the front step in the bright sunlight, surveying his new surroundings, when Father hopped across the front lawn, only a few feet away. Mr. Muldoon merely eyed him indolently and continued to survey the landscape. Uncle Analdas then tried, and although he did not kick him in the face as he had threatened, he did run close enough to throw some dirt on him. The old Cat shook it off, yawned, and went to sleep.

Emboldened by this, Willie Fieldmouse and several of his cousins gathered around in a semicircle, jeering and making faces. They hopped up and down and sang insultingly:

> *Mr. Muldoon*
> *Is a raccoon,*
> *Phew! Phew! Phew!*

But Mr. Muldoon just put a paw over his ear and continued to slumber.

"Shucks," grunted Uncle Analdas, "he couldn't danger *nobody.*"

Father of course was eager to discover if the newcomers were truly gentlefolk, for he laid great store by good manners and breeding. It was not until late afternoon, however, that an opportunity offered. The Folks had gone out in the car, so Father with a few of his friends waited patiently beside the drive until their return. As the car rumbled up the driveway he skipped across, directly in front of the oncoming wheels.

The Man slammed on his brakes and came to a full stop. Then he and the Lady both raised their hats and recited in unison, "Good evening, sir, and good luck to you," replaced their hats, and drove on, slowly and carefully.

Father was tremendously pleased. "Now there," he announced to the other Animals, "there is real gentility and good breeding for you. Not that I wish to cast aspersions on the manners of the Folk of this, my adopted State, but I must say that this is the first time since my residence here that I have encountered this pleasant and considerate custom which, where I was reared, is universally observed. Now down in the Bluegrass—"

"Oh, you and your bluegrass," snorted Phewie. "I ain't interested in their manners. What *I'm* interested in is their garbidge."

"You will find, Phewie," said Father with some heat, "that good breeding and good garbage go hand in hand."

Their argument was interrupted by the pipe-smell which always preceded the Man. He was coming down the drive carrying a neat wooden sign fastened to a stake, a crowbar, a hammer, and various other implements. They all watched intently while he proceeded to erect the sign just inside the driveway entrance.

"What's it say, Georgie? Read it off to me," whispered Uncle Analdas. "Seem to've mislaid them dingblasted spectacles."

Little Georgie spelled it out. "It says, *Please—drive—carefully—on—account—of—Small—Animals.*"

"Well naow! I calls that real nice," admitted Uncle Analdas. "Your maw will certainly be pleased to hear about that, Georgie. *Please drive careful account o' Small Animals.* Yes *sir,* that's real thoughtful."

In various other ways the new Folks soon began to measure up to the high standards which the Little Animals had set for nice people. To a group of cronies gathered on the hillside the Gray Fox cited an incident which had heightened his approval.

"Real sensible, knowledgeable Folks they seem to be," he said. "Quiet-like and friendly. Why just yesterday afternoon late I was prospecting around, sort of smelled chicken frying, I guess, and I came through that little walled-in garden where the benches are. I wasn't paying much attention, and he, the Man, wasn't smoking his pipe or I'd have known he was around, when first thing I knew there I was right in front of him, face to face you might say. He was reading a book and he looked up, and what do you suppose he did? Nothing, that's what. He just sat there and looked at me, and I stood there and looked at him, and then he said, 'Oh, hello,' and went back to reading his book, and I went on about *my* business. Now that's the sort of Folks *is* Folks."

"And *her*," grunted Porkey, nodding approvingly. "Any of you hear that ruckus went on the other afternoon? Well, sir, I was pokin' around out there in the field, careless-like too, I guess, way out in the open and too early in the day, when all of a sudden that there biggest Dog from

Down-to-the-Crossroads was right on me. 'Course I wasn't *scared* but I *was* in a bad fix, not havin' nothin' to get my back against, so I just rares up and dares him to come on and git it. He's wearin' a couple of rips on his nose already I gave him two-three years ago, so he dassent come in, but starts circlin', tryin' to git behind me. And there he is, a-bellerin' and a-roarin' and a-rushin', when *she* steps out of the garden where she'd been a-workin', with a rock in her hand the size of a mushmelon.

"She takes a good look at the situation, she sets her feet solid, and then she hauls off and *wham* she lets him have it! Right in the ribs it took him, and man, man! the yawp that Mongrel let out you could have heard clear over to Charcoal Hill!"

"You could," Father agreed. "I did. It just happened I was visiting our daughter Hazel at her Charcoal Hill residence that very afternoon and heard the howls with the utmost distinctness—and no little pleasure."

"And what did *she* do?" Porkey went on. "Why she just dusts her hands, looks at me calm as you please, and grins and says, 'Why don't you keep your eyes open, stupid?' and goes back to her diggin'. Now I ain't never lived in no bluegrass region, so I don't know nothin' about aristocrats and gentilities and them things, but what I hold is this—and I

[80]

dare anybody to contradict it — " he pounded the earth and glared belligerently around the small circle — "*I* hold that anybody can heave a rock like that is a *Lady!*"

Then there was the slight argument about Porkey's burrow. Slight, perhaps, in the eyes of Folks, but of great significance to the Animals.

Louie Kernstawk was rebuilding the stone wall where Porkey's burrow lay. When he came near the entrance the

Man had said, "Let's just leave that piece of wall, Mr. Kernstawk; there's a Woodchuck living under there and we really shouldn't disturb him."

"Leave it?" exclaimed Louie, astonished. "Why you can't leave that Groundhog live there. He'll just ruin your garden. I was figurin' on bringing up my shotgun and getting him tomorrow."

"No. No shooting," said the Man firmly.

"I could set a trap for him," Louie suggested.

"No. No traps." The Lady spoke just as firmly.

Louie scratched his head in puzzlement. "Well, of course it's your place and if that's the way you want it, okay," he said, "but it's going to look awful funny, that old tumbledown hunk of wall right in the middle of this new builtup one."

"Oh, I guess it will be all right." The Man laughed as they moved on.

Louie was still scratching his head when Tim McGrath wandered over. "What did I tell you about folks that read books too much?" Tim demanded. "Makes 'em queer, that's what it does. Why here's these people, as nice, pleasant-spoken people as you could want—but queer. Only yesterday I was telling them they'd have to get rid of these here moles. Said I'd bring up a couple of my traps and set 'em, and she sez quick, just like she sez to you, 'No. No traps.' So I sez I'd got some good poison I could put out and *he* sez, 'No. No poison.'

"'Well how in thunder then, I sez, can I make you a half-way decent lawn with them there moles rootin' around into it?' And what do you suppose he sez to that? 'Oh, just keep a-rollin' it down,' he sez, 'just keep rollin' it and they'll git discouraged.' *Discouraged,* mind you!" Tim snorted. "Sez he read it in a book.

"And then, only this morning," he went on, "I was telling them they'd ought to build a fence around that garden. 'Why, you can't never have no garden here, I sez, without you have a fence around it. This here Hill is full of Animals; Rabbits, Groundhogs, Raccoons, Deer, Pheasants, Skunks, and all.' And what do you suppose she sez to that?"

"I couldn't imagine," answered Louie.

"You couldn't," said Tim. "'We like 'em,' she sez. 'They're so beautiful,' she sez. *Beautiful,* mind you! 'And *they* must be hungry too,' sez she.

"'You're right, ma'am,' I sez. 'They're hungry all right, as you'll learn to your sorrow,' I sez, 'when them vegetables come up.'

"And then *he* chips in, the man. 'Oh, I guess we'll get along all right with 'em,' sez he. 'I think there'll be enough

[83]

for all of us—' *us*, mind you. 'That's why we planned the garden so big,' he sez."

Tim shook his head sadly. "Seems a shame, nice folks too, pleasant-spoken and all—but queer. Nuts, some might say. Comes of readin' books too much, I guess. Grandpa had the right of it. 'Readin' rots the mind,' *he* used to say."

Louie picked up his hammer and split a stone neatly. "Nice folks, though," he said. "Seems too bad."

Willie Fieldmouse was sent to observe the new Folks each evening, not in any spirit of impertinent prying, of course, but naturally the Little Animals were interested in knowing what things were being planned for the Hill, for after all, it was *their* Hill.

There was a rainwater barrel near the living-room window, and by climbing to the top of this Willie was able to jump to the window sill. Although the evenings were still cool and a fire crackled on the hearth, the window was usually opened slightly. Seated in a dark shadow on the sill, he could safely observe the Folks and listen to their garden plans. Tonight, surrounded by a sea of catalogs, they had been making out their lists of seeds and plants.

Willie had tried very hard to remember them all and was now making his report. Seated outside the rabbit burrow, Mother, Father, Uncle Analdas, Phewie, Porkey, and several others all listened intently.

"There's radishes," Willie recited, ticking them off on his claws, "carrots, peas, beans — snap and lima — lettuce — "

"Peavine and lettuce soup," sighed Mother happily.

"Corn, spinach, kale, turnips, kohl-rabi, broccoli — "

"Don't hold with them foreign vittles," Uncle Analdas grumbled, but was hushed by Mother, and Willie went on. "Celery, rhubarb, potatoes, tomatoes, peppers, cabbage — red and white — cauliflower, raspberries — black and red — strawberries, melons, asparagus — and that's all I can remember — oh yes, cucumbers and squash."

[85]

A happy buzz of excitement swept over the gathering as Willie finished his report and took a deep breath. The conversation soon merged into a series of arguments as to which families should have which vegetables, but quieted down when Father rose and rapped for attention.

"As you well know," he said firmly, "it has always been our custom here on the Hill to settle all such questions on Dividing Night, which falls this year, I believe, on May 26. On that evening we shall, as usual, gather at the garden and allot to each Animal and his family those vegetables to which they are entitled by rule and taste."

"Where do I come in?" Uncle Analdas demanded. "I'm just a-visitin' here."

"As our house guest," answered Father, "you will of course receive the customary allotment."

"Gumdinged right I will," said Uncle Analdas.

RL

8. Willie's Bad Night

IT WAS bluegrass that almost proved the undoing of
Willie Fieldmouse. He was on the window sill, as usual,
watching and listening to the Folks. This evening, having
finished their gardening plans, they were talking of grass
seed. Willie was not especially interested and was only half
listening when he was suddenly electrified by a familiar
word.

"This book," the Man was saying, "recommends a mix-
ture of red top, white clover, and Kentucky bluegrass."

Bluegrass! Kentucky bluegrass! Wouldn't Father Rabbit
be pleased! He must be told at once!

[87]

Haste and excitement made Willie inexcusably careless. He should have remembered that the lid of the rainwater barrel was old and rotted, that there were several dangerous holes in it. He did not, and his leap from the window sill landed him squarely in one of the holes. He grabbed frantically as he went through, but the rotten wood crumbled under his claws and with a sickening shock he plunged into the icy water.

He came up gasping. The cold seemed to have driven all the air from his lungs but he managed one wild squeak for help before the water closed over him again. He was very feeble when he came up this time. He struggled weakly toward the side of the barrel, but the walls were slippery with moss and his paws too numbed to get a hold. Faintly he squeaked once more—why didn't someone help him, Father or Little Georgie or Phewie? As the water closed over him for the last time he was dimly conscious of a noise and a brilliant glare of light. Then the light went out, everything went out.

A long time later, he never knew how long, Willie's eyes fluttered open. He dimly realized that he was still wet, that uncontrollable fits of shivering shook him. He seemed to be lying in a nest of some soft white stuff which was very comfortable; he could see the glow of dancing flames and feel a gentle warmth. Then he closed his eyes again.

Later they opened and he saw the faces of the Folks bending over his bed. It was terrifying to see Folks this close. They looked enormous, like something in a night-mare. He tried to burrow into the soft cotton when his nose suddenly caught the smell of warm milk. Someone was holding a medicine dropper before his face. On the end of it a white drop hung. Weakly Willie licked at it — it was delicious. There was something else in the milk, something that coursed hotly through all his body. He felt stronger already and sucked at the dropper until it was completely empty. Ah, that was better! His stomach was swollen with the comforting warm food; his eyelids drooped, and again he slept.

There was consternation among the Animals when Willie failed to report to the group waiting at the burrow. Father and Uncle Analdas immediately organized a searching party but were unable to find any trace of him.

Phewie, who had been enjoying the freedom of the garbage pail, reported that he had heard a mouse-cry, had seen the Folks emerge from the house with flashlights and do something at the rain barrel. Just what, he did not know.

Willie's oldest cousin climbed to the window sill but found the window closed. The Gray Squirrel was wakened and sent to the roof to investigate. He listened at all the upstairs windows without discovering anything unusual.

"It's that dingblasted old Cat," shouted Uncle Analdas. "The sneakin', deceitful, hypocritical scoundrel, makin' out he's old and harmless. Wish I'd kicked him in the face like I planned to."

Porkey was inclined to blame Tim McGrath. "It's him and his traps," he argued. "Always talkin' traps he is, and poisons. Likely he led them Folks into settin' a trap fer Willie."

Father said little, but all the night through he, Uncle Analdas, and Little Georgie coursed the Hill like Setter Dogs, searching every inch of field and wall, looking under every shrub and bush. Not till dawn approached did they admit defeat and return wearily to the burrow, where Mother, very red-eyed and sniffly, had a hot breakfast waiting for them.

But of all the Animals the Mole's rage and grief were the

most moving. His pal, his eyes, was lost and he was help-less to join in the search!

"I'll fix 'em," he said grimly. "I'll fix 'em. There won't never a blade of grass take root on this place—never! Never a bulb or a shrub stay set neither. I'll tear 'em up and I'll root 'em out, I'll dig and I'll heave and I'll burrow, I'll fetch in every friend and relation from here to Danbury way and tear this place apart till they wish they'd never—"

His threats were muffled as he plunged frantically into the neatly rolled front lawn. All night the other Animals could hear his grunting, could see the surface of the ground ripple and heave like troubled waters.

It was gray dawn when Willie woke again. The room was chilly but on the hearth a few embers still smoldered, and the bricks gave out a comforting warmth. He eased him-self out of the cardboard box where he had slept and drew closer to the glowing coals. All his muscles felt stiff and sore; he was still a little wobbly but otherwise he felt very well. He bathed a bit and stretched himself, feeling better all the time. That warm milk and whatever was in it had certainly tasted good. He wished he had some more. He ought to be getting along home but there was no way out —the doors and windows were all closed.

The sun had risen before he heard footsteps approaching through the house. He caught a whiff of the Man's pipe smell, heard the soft pad of Mr. Muldoon's paws. Wildly he looked for a hiding place; but no good one offered. On either side of the fireplace bookshelves extended from floor to ceiling, and in desperation he leaped to the top of the first row of books and crouched back into the darkest corner just as the door opened.

The Folks came in and at once inspected the box. "Well, well, he's gone," said the Man. "Must be feeling better. Wonder where he is?"

The Lady did not answer. She was watching Mr. Muldoon, who had wandered idly over to the bookshelves.

Willie backed as far into the corner as he could squeeze, his heart pounding wildly as the great Cat drew closer and

RL

closer. The head seemed huge now, the mouth was opening, two rows of white fangs showed, his eyes were gleam-
ing yellow coals. Willie, petrified with fear, could only
watch helplessly as the red jaws opened wider and wider.
He could feel the hot breath, strong with the odor of canned
salmon.

Then Mr. Muldoon sneezed.

"There he is," the Lady said quietly, "on the books, in
the corner. Come, Mullie, don't worry the poor little thing.
He's had enough trouble already." She seated herself, and
the Cat strolled stiffly over, leaped to her lap, and settled
down for a nap. The Man opened the outside door and also
sat down.

It was some time before Willie's breath came back and
his heart returned to normal. When it did he ventured forth,
an inch at a time. Nothing happened, so he began the long
circuit of the room, staying close to the wall and pausing
under each piece of furniture. He was almost to the doorway now and gave one quick survey before the final dash.

The Lady still continued to sit quietly, her fingers slowly
stroking Mr. Muldoon's jowls. He snored faintly, with a
sound not unlike the steady, gurgling wheeze of the Man's
pipe.

One wild scurry and Willie burst out into the sunlight.

[93]

Across the terrace he went, but even in the excitement of his newly won freedom he was forced to pause at the appearance of the front lawn. The smoothly rolled surface was striped and circled and crisscrossed with a perfect crazy-quilt pattern of mole runs, scarcely a foot of it undisturbed. He skipped to the nearest run, made two digs, and plunged beneath the surface.

"Mole! Mole!" he cried as he galloped through the echoing tunnel. "Here I am, Mole, it's me — Little Willie."

Tim McGrath, hands on hips, stood on the front lawn, surveying the wreckage of his careful labor. His jaws were a deep, purplish red; his neck seemed swollen with suppressed rage.

"Look at it!" he sputtered. "*Just look at it!* What did I tell you about them moles? But no. No traps, of course not. No poison, oh dear me, no! *Now look!*"

The Man sucked on his pipe rather apologetically. "It *is* quite a mess, isn't it?" he admitted. "I guess we'll just have to roll it down again."

Tim McGrath gazed at the sky and whispered softly, "*We'll* have to roll it again! *We'll have to roll it again!* Oh Lord, give me strength." Wearily he trudged away to fetch the rake and roller.

9. Dividing Night

THE DAYS lengthened and the sun climbed higher, and with the lengthening days the spirits of the Little Animals also rose. In the garden long rows of brilliant green vegetables were thrusting their way up. The lawns were now rich carpets of new grass, very smooth and beautiful, for the Mole, ashamed of his destructive rampage, had kept strictly away from them. Each evening Father inspected the bluegrass. It was slow-growing and would not amount to much this year, but next summer—oh my! From his burrow entrance Porkey surveyed the flourishing field of buckwheat with great satisfaction.

In the chicken-run countless baby chicks ran and scratched and peeped endlessly while the mother hens chuckled and scolded. Phewie and the Gray Fox often paused there in the early evenings to look over the prospects, but Phewie was so satisfied by Sulphronia's generosity in the matter of garbage that his interest in live chicken was rapidly waning. He had even persuaded the Fox to sample a bit of her cookery. The Fox at first had scorned the idea, saying he preferred his chicken fresh, but after trying a Southern-fried chicken wing, as Sulphronia fried it, he had been quite won over and now usually joined Phewie in his midnight feasts.

Each evening the Animals inspected the garden. The seed packets placed on sticks at the ends of the rows were all gone over carefully with many ohs and ahs at the brightly colored pictures. Little Georgie, of course, had to read them for Uncle Analdas, who had always mislaid his specs.

Each Animal made notes on the vegetables available and his family's tastes and needs, in preparation for Dividing Night.

That long-awaited occasion arrived and passed off with less controversy than usual, for the garden was so large that there seemed to be ample for all, even the most finicky.

It was a bright moonlit night, and every Animal on the Hill had gathered to present his claims. Phewie and the Gray Fox acted as judges, for, not being vegetarians, they could be trusted to make fair and disinterested decisions. Father, of course, made most of the speeches.

One question arose which had never come up at any former Dividing Night. Willie Fieldmouse and his relatives, grateful for the Folks' rescue of Willie from the rain barrel, proposed that a small portion of the garden be set aside for the exclusive use of the household. Mother warmly seconded this, for she had been most touched by the sign on the driveway. There was considerable debate, but Porkey seemed to represent the opinion of the majority

[97]

when he said, "Let them take their chances along with the rest of us. Folks don't respect our claims, so why should we give *them* special privileges. 'Tain't democratic." So the motion was voted down.

To some present, Uncle Analdas' claims seemed a little extravagant. After all, he was not a regular resident of the Hill, but since he was the guest of Father and Mother, both of whom were highly regarded, there was no open comment, although there was a bit of spiteful gossip behind cupped paws.

On the whole the meeting was most pleasant and orderly, very different from some of the former ones, when the meager, ill-kept gardens of the previous Folks had led to a great deal of wrangling.

Father voiced this thought in his closing speech. "We seem," he said, "to be blessed with most generous, well-bred and kindly Folks. Their present plantings promise the most bountiful garden with which we have been favored in many years. I hope, therefore, that it is not necessary to impress on any of you the desirability of adhering strictly to those rules and regulations which have always been observed here on the Hill.

"Each Animal's allotment shall be for his and his family's exclusive use and enjoyment; anyone encroaching on

property not his own risks banishment from our community.

"In the event that the Folks should take an undue quantity of vegetables from any one Animal's holding, our Board of Relief will assign him additional space.

"Finally, *nothing is to be touched until Midsummer's Eve.* This rule is of the utmost importance, for we have learned by long experience that premature inroads on the crops only result in hardship for everyone. By allowing them to approach maturity a far more plentiful supply will be available for all. I hope that you will all use that patience and self-restraint for which the Animals of our Hill have long been noted and that those of us whose duty it is to see that these regulations are enforced will not be called upon to invoke any disciplinary measures. May I also remind you, Porkey, and you, Foxy, that this prohibition applies to buckwheat, chickens, and ducks, as well as vegetables?"

"It's all right with *me*," Phewie piped up. "Ain't no closed season on garbidge. Come on, Foxy, this is fried-chicken night. I move the meetin's adjourned."

The Animals all wandered home from the meeting in a most contented mood. A group of the young ones were singing "Happy Days Are Here Again." Of course it was quite a wait to Midsummer's Eve, but the fields were green now, there was plenty of natural provender, and the garden promised a really bumper crop. The housewives were all planning their preserving and canning. Mother broached the subject of a new storage room which she had long desired. Uncle Analdas could help with the excavating, and

Little Georgie had become quite handy with tools now, so he could build the shelves. Little Georgie had been sent to the Fat-Man-at-the-Crossroads for some items overlooked in the morning's marketing, and, seated before the burrow, Mother went on outlining her plans for the storeroom.

Suddenly the night air was rent by that hideous sound that brings a chill of dread to the hearts of all country dwellers — the long, rising shriek of car brakes, the whine of slithering tires. There was a moment of frozen silence, then from the Black Road a man's curse, a motor roaring into new life, and a car going on.

Mother gave one gasp—"Georgie!"—and collapsed, but Father and Uncle Analdas streaked for the road. They could hear the tearing of bushes as the Red Buck thundered down the Hill, could hear Porkey's wheezing gallop, the twitterings of the hastening Fieldmice.

But fast as they all were, the Folks from the house were faster. Father could hear their running footsteps on the gravel drive, see the blue-white gleam of a flashlight.

The Animals crowded the bushes, peering out at the dreaded Black Road where the Folks bent over a small, limp object. They heard the Man say, "Here, hold the flashlight," saw him whip off his coat and spread it on the roadway, heard him say, "There now, there now" as, kneeling, he gently wrapped something in it. They saw him tramp up the driveway, carrying the bundle carefully. They saw the Lady's face, white and drawn in the moonlight, and they heard her saying things no Lady should ever say.

10. Clouds Over the Hill

BLACK grief wrapped the Hill, for of all the younger Animals Little Georgie was the most beloved. His cheerfulness and youthful enthusiasm had always brightened the days for the older ones, his unfailing willingness had made him invaluable to Mother. For Father he had been an apt pupil and a congenial hunting companion. The long runs they had had together, the many times they had outwitted and tricked blundering Dogs, all came rushing back now and overwhelmed poor Father with inconsolable sorrow.

Mother had taken to her bed, and their daughter Hazel had been summoned from over Charcoal Hill way to take over the running of the household. She was not a very good cook and had brought along three of her youngest children. Their senseless chatter drove Uncle Analdas frantic and he avoided the burrow as much as possible, spending long, gloomy hours with Phewie, Porkey, or the Red Buck.

"What a runner he was," said the Buck sadly. "What a runner. Many's the time he'd run with me clear up Weston way, not on business, just for the fun of it. Up there and back before breakfast, and him real young too. Sometimes I'd say, 'Are you tiring, Georgie?' and he'd only laugh. 'Tiring?' he'd say. 'Only just warming up'—and away he'd go. Made me stretch, times, to keep up."

"And a leaper," said Uncle Analdas. "Clear 'cross Deadman's Brook he lep. Seen the spot with my own eyes—a good eighteen foot if it's an inch. Ain't no Rabbit ever done the like of that before. Won't be another one likely, neither."

Porkey shook his head. "Cheerful too. Always a-laughin' and a-singin'. Don't seem right."

"Them dingblasted automobiles," Uncle Analdas raged. "I'll fix 'em! I'll get 'em. Wait till there comes a good rainy night with that dingblasted Black Road all a-slimy and

a-slippery. I'll hide me down at the curve there near the bottom of the Hill and when they come a-rampagin' and a-roarin' along I'll skip across in front of 'em. That'll wake 'em up! You'll see 'em slam on their brakes and go a-skiddin' and a-slitherin' and a-slidin' and a-crashin' into that there stone wall.

"Used to do it up Danbury way when I was younger, just fer cussedness. Four cars I wrecked on that hill up there, three of 'em real bad. Too old now, though." He sighed helplessly. "Ain't spry enough. They'd get me sure."

They sat in sad silence while the shadow of the Pine Wood crept slowly down the Hill, until the setting sun turned the buckwheat to a carpet of shimmering green-gold. "Always used to come a-runnin' by, 'bout this time," Porkey said. "Always called, 'Good evenin', Mr. Porkey.' Well brung up, he was. Always called me 'Mister.' It just don't seem right."

Even the approach of Midsummer's Eve did little to lift the gloom. The Animals watched the garden's progress with only a half-hearted interest. Feathery carrot tops, tender peavines with their succulent tendrils, fresh young lettuce beginning to head, jade-like cabbages, stout rows of beans —all these would formerly have been noted with ecstasy, but now no one seemed to care much.

To Father the coming Eve promised more of unhappiness than pleasure, for they had planned to have a little celebration this year, he and Mother, a sort of Harvest Home after the storage room had been filled. All the neighbors would come in, there would be peavine and lettuce soup, and there were still a few small bottles of elderflower wine buried away. There would be games and laughter and singing, it would be just like the good old days — it would have been.

The new storeroom had not been built. He and Uncle Analdas had no heart for it — and Little Georgie was to have made the shelves. Mother had made no plans for preserving or canning. She had only recently been able to sit up in her rocker.

Father sat outside the burrow in the twilight; the incessant chatter of the youngsters made indoors impossible.

Hazel herself was noisy and careless with the dishes. Near by, Uncle Analdas napped fitfully.

Suddenly Father became aware of a small crowd hastening down the Hill. He could hear Willie Fieldmouse's excited voice, the squeaking of his cousins. He could see Phewie's bright black and white and distinguish Porkey's waddling bulk. As they neared the burrow Willie broke from the rest and came galloping toward them, his voice squealing in excitement.

"I've seen him!" he called wildly. "I've seen him! Uncle Analdas, wake up, I've seen him—I've seen Little Georgie!"

Bedlam broke loose. Hazel rushed to the doorway, her hands dripping dishwater; her three young ones yelled louder than ever; the Fieldmice twittered frantically. Mother tottered from her chair, and Uncle Analdas fell backward out of his. "Hush them blasted brats," he roared, scrambling to his feet. "How can anybody—" Everyone screamed questions at once.

Phewie stamped the ground with his front paws. "Silence!" he shouted. His plumy tail arched ever so slightly. "The first one says another word, I'll—" Silence fell at once, for Phewie never made idle threats. "Now, Willie," he said quietly, "go on with your story."

"Well," said Willie breathlessly, "I was on the window

sill — there's a new cover on the rain barrel and I wanted to try it and I did and it's a good stout one too — I was on the window sill and I looked in and I saw him — I saw Little Georgie! He was lying in her lap, the Lady's, right in her lap an'—"

"Haow 'bout that dingblasted old Cat?" interrupted Uncle Analdas. "Where was he?"

"He was there, he was there too, and — *he was washing Little Georgie's face!*"

At this such an incredulous chattering broke out that Phewie was forced to arch his tail again.

"He was too, he really was," Willie went on, "ears and all. And Georgie seemed to like it and once he bent his head down and Mr. Muldoon, the Cat, you know, he scratched the back of Georgie's neck for him."

"Flea, likely," said Uncle Analdas.

"And that's all I saw and I thought you ought to know, so I came right away — and that's all."

"Was he — did he seem — all right?" Mother asked breathlessly.

Willie hesitated a moment. "Well he — seemed to — well, his hind legs, his jumping ones, seemed to be tied up, sort of — with little sticks, like, and bandages."

"Could he walk?" asked Father quickly.

"Well, I don't exactly know, sir. You see, he was just lying in her lap, the Lady's lap—and I don't know—but he seemed real comfortable and happy like."

"Thank you, William," said Father. "You are a good boy and a very observant and thoughtful one. We are overjoyed at your tidings and are deeply grateful. Anything further that you are able to discover we shall look forward to with the greatest eagerness."

Relief and joy burst out in a flood of chatter, of questions and speculation. The glad news spread rapidly over the Hill, and the gloom that had hung there began to dissolve like the morning mist.

Everyone dropped in to offer congratulations. Mother, of course, was still worried, but there was a light in her eyes that had not been there since that terrible night. They filled with tears, however, when Porkey—old Porkey, the shy and solitary, always ill at ease in social gatherings—waddled awkwardly up and offered his gnarled, clay-encrusted paw. "Ma'am," he said gruffly. "Ma'am, I—we—er—*aw shucks*" —and he hastened away.

11. Strain and Strife

BRIGHT and early next morning Father and Uncle Analdas started work on the new storeroom. The gloomy lethargy that had wrapped all the residents of the Hill was completely gone; Mother bustled cheerily about her housework, at times even humming a bar or two of Little Georgie's song. Hazel and her three chatterers were sent home with many thanks from Mother and Father and ill-concealed pleasure on the part of Uncle Analdas. "Now maybe a feller can get a rest once in a while, 'thout havin' his dingblasted ears shouted off," he grunted, shoveling busily.

As the days went by and the storeroom progressed, only one worry marred the general happiness. Willie Fieldmouse had never been able to catch another glimpse of Little Georgie.

Each night he faithfully climbed the rain barrel and peered into the living room, but the Folks had an upstairs sitting room now and seemed to spend most of their evenings there. All the Animals kept their eyes and ears open, but none ever heard or saw a trace of Little Georgie.

That he was still there they felt sure, for early each morning the Lady gathered a small basket of dew-soaked clover, carrot tops, fresh young lettuce leaves, or tender peavines. From the quantity she gathered they judged not only that Georgie was there but that his appetite was excellent.

The days merged into weeks with still no news. Midsummer's Eve was not far off, and the mounting anxiety caused tempers to grow short. In the case of Father and Uncle Analdas this irritability was increased by their unskilled attempts at carpentry. The storeroom shelves which Little Georgie could have built so easily took them days and days and cost many pounded paws. When finished, the lopsided and rickety results seemed hardly worth the pain and labor they had spent on them.

After pounding his thumb for the fourth time in succession Uncle Analdas threw down his hammer in a rage and went off to visit with Porkey. Irritation and worry had gradually caused a dark suspicion to take root in his mind, and he now proceeded to voice it.

"D'ye know," he said, "I don't trust these here new Folks, not none. I'm plumb worried about Little Georgie. D'ye know what I think? What *I* think is they're a-holdin' him fer a hostage, that's what they're doin'. Mark my words now, come Midsummer night and the first time ary one of us touches ary one of their dingblasted vegetables they'll a-torture him, that's what they'll do—or maybe do away with him complete.

"They may be a-torturin' him right now," he went on gloomily, "a-torturin' an' a-teasin' an' a-pryin', an' a-tryin' to make him tell all about *us*, where our burrows is and all, so's they kin set out poison an' traps an' spring-guns. And how about them sticks tied onto his legs Willie was tellin' about? Some kind of torture machines likely. Nossir, I don't trust 'em. Don't trust that dingblasted old Cat neither. I'll kick him in the face yet."

Uncle Analdas' suspicions of foul play rapidly spread

among the other Animals and soon resulted in a bitter controversy. Mother and Father and the Red Buck refused to
believe anything so evil of the new Folks and were sup-
ported by the Gray Fox and Phewie, who both felt sure
that Folks who set out such bountiful garbage must be in
all ways kind and good.

But many of the other Animals were inclined to side with
Uncle Analdas. Arguments and quarrels grew more and
more frequent. As usual, many wild and sinister rumors
were circulated. Lights had been seen in the Folks' sitting
room at late hours. Strange sounds had been heard. The
Opossum, a notorious liar, claimed to have heard Little
Georgie screaming in pain.

To make things worse, the spring rains came. Day after
day the low-hanging black clouds came scudding in from
the east, rolling across the valley and spilling incessant

[114]

showers. A chilling northeast wind blew; mist and damp-
ness seeped down into the best-built burrows. On the walls
mildew and fungus appeared; roofs leaked and chimneys
smoked. The housebound Animals shivered and hugged
their hearths. It was good weather for gardens but bad for
dispositions.

Each day, through mud and drizzle, Father tramped the
Hill seeking tidings of Little Georgie, returning drenched,
mud-spattered, and somber. All day Uncle Analdas
crouched over the fire, smoking his reeking pipe and mut-
tering wild and gloomy forebodings. It was only natural
that they should eventually quarrel. Bitter words were
spoken, Mother wept as copiously as the driving clouds,
and Uncle Analdas wrathfully stamped from the burrow to
take up his abode with Porkey. There he became the ring-
leader of the rebellious element and spent his days adding
fuel to the fires of suspicion and hate.

Even Porkey had to admit that he seemed to be slightly
"tetched," but the more ignorant Animals eagerly swallowed
every fantastic suspicion and became more and more
worked up. Some of the more violent even suggested that
the rules of the Hill be thrown aside and that without waiting for Midsummer's Eve they at once lay waste the gardens and lawns, the buckwheat field and the flower borders,

that they ruthlessly slaughter every chick and duckling, every hen and rooster.

At a painfully stormy meeting it required all Father's eloquence and all the Red Buck's authority to persuade the Animals to abide by their ancient rules and customs. A shift in the wind and clearing weather also helped somewhat in soothing frayed nerves and strained relations.

For some time now Louie Kernstawk had been working at something up near the end of the garden. It was a lovely spot, a tiny circular lawn sheltered by a great pine tree and sloping down into the rock garden. There were two stone benches there where the Folks often sat on warm evenings, a custom which prevented the Animals from thoroughly inspecting Louie's handiwork.

There was considerable speculation as to what it could be, but Uncle Analdas soon had an explanation for it.

"They're a-buildin' a dungeon," he shouted. "They're a-buildin' a dungeon fer Little Georgie, that's what they're a-doin'. And they'll put him into it behind big iron bars and he'll be a-pinin' there and every time ary one of us touches a dingblasted vegetable they'll a-torture him and jab him and starve him — and maybe pour boilin' oil onto him!"

So Midsummer's Eve drew near in a seething atmosphere of suspicion, fear, and general unpleasantness. This was all added to by the arrival of a long and very heavy wooden packing case.

It came on Tim McGrath's truck, and it took the combined efforts of Tim, Louie, the Man, and several helpers to unload it and move it on rollers to the little lawn under the pine tree where Louie's work was going on. At once Uncle Analdas started a new rumor. "Traps and spring-guns," he announced, "that's what's in that there box. Traps and spring-guns and likely poisons and gases."

Whatever was in it was unpacked with a great deal of hammering. Louie and his helpers were very busy for a day or two more, with the Folks continually stirring around and in and out. It was not until the afternoon of the Eve that the work was finished. Everything was cleaned up neatly, and whatever had been done was covered by one of Louie's canvas tarpaulins. Something stood up in the center, making the canvas look rather like a tent as it shone there in the sunset light.

Porkey and Uncle Analdas regarded it suspiciously from a safe distance up the hillside.

"It's a gallows," Uncle Analdas pronounced in a sepulchral whisper. "It's a gallows, that's what it is, and they're a-goin' to hang poor Little Georgie onto it."

12. There Is Enough for All

THE SUN had set, and the gold of the west slowly faded to a cool clear green. Venus, hanging low over the Pine Wood, burned brilliantly, all alone at first, but as the sky deepened the smaller stars began to show themselves. High up the new moon swam like a silver sickle.

As the dusk thickened the whole Hill began to whisper with the soft rustle of small bodies passing through the grass, with the swish of tiny feet, all making their way toward the garden, for this was Midsummer's Eve and the Little Animals were gathering.

On the edge of the small circular lawn the Folks sat silently. It was dark and shadowy here under the big pine. All that could be seen was the dim whiteness of the stone benches, the regular glowing and dying of the Man's pipe, and the tent-like, gray tarpaulin. The top of this glowed in the moon's pale light like a beacon, and like a beacon it seemed to beckon all the Animals, for instead of gathering at the garden they were all pressing closer and closer to the little round lawn. Slowly, silently, one step at a time, they moved through the deep grass and the shrub shadows until the clearing was entirely surrounded by an audience of small, tense Animals, waiting for—they knew not what.

The moonlight was brighter now; the little lawn was like a small, lighted stage. They could make out the Lady sitting motionless on the bench, beside her the drowsing bulk of Mr. Muldoon. It was so still that they could hear his wheezy breathing.

Suddenly the silence was rudely shattered by Uncle Analdas' harsh cry as he stepped shakily into the open. His sunken eyes were staring, his ears cocked at crazy angles.

"Where is he?" he croaked wildly. "Where is he? Where's

that dingblasted old Cat? Leave me at him! They're not a-goin' to hang our Little Georgie!"

Mother sprang from the shadows, calling, "Analdas, come back. Oh, stop him, someone, stop him!"

There was a sudden stir in the Lady's lap; then, clear and joyous, Little Georgie's voice rang out. "Mother," it cried. A small form sprang to the ground and sped across the clearing. "Mother, Father, it's me, Little Georgie, I'm all well — look at me — look —"

In the bright moonlight he leaped and cavorted on the lawn, around and across, up and down, over and over. He jumped high over Uncle Analdas and turned a double handspring. He sprang to the bench and kicked Mr. Muldoon playfully in the stomach. The old Cat lazily caught him round the waist and they wrestled happily, finally falling to the ground with a thump. Remembering his age and dignity, Muldoon clambered back onto the bench, where his purr rumbled like a far off gristmill.

A joyous chattering broke out among the Animals, but stilled when the Man quietly rose and approached the tarpaulin. Very deliberately he loosed its fastenings and flung it clear. In the deep silence that followed it was almost possible to hear the sound of a hundred little breaths caught and released in a sigh of awe.

The Mole grasped Willie Fieldmouse's elbow. "Willie, what is it?" he whispered. "What is it? *Willie, be eyes for me.*"

Willie's voice was hushed and breathless. "Oh, Mole," he said. "Oh, Mole, it's so beautiful. It's him, Mole, it's *him*—the Good Saint!"

"Him—of Assisi?" asked the Mole.

"Yes, Mole, *our* Saint. The good St. Francis of Assisi—him that's loved us and protected us Little Animals time out of mind—and, oh, Mole, it's so beautiful! He's all out of stone, Mole, and his face is so kind and so sad. He's got a long robe on, old and poor like, you can see the patches on it.

"And all around his feet are the Little Animals. They're *us*, Mole, all out of stone. There's you and me and there's all the Birds and there's Little Georgie and Porkey and the Fox—even old Lumpy the Hop Toad. And the Saint's hands are held out in front of him sort of kind—like blessing things. And from his hands there's water dropping, Mole, clear, cool water. It drops into a pool there in front of him."

"I can hear it splashing," the Mole whispered, "and I can smell the good clear pool and feel its coolness. Go on, Willie, be eyes for me."

"It's a fine pool for drinking of, Mole, and at each end

it's shallow like, so the Birds can bathe there. And, oh, Mole, all around the pool is broad flat stones, a sort of rim, like a shelf or something, and it's all set out with things to eat, like a banquet feast. And there's letters, there's words onto it, Mole, cut in the stones."

"What does it say, Willie, the printing?"

Willie spelled it out slowly, carefully. "It says — *There — is — enough — for — all.*' There's enough for all, Mole. And there *is*.

"There's grain — corn and wheat and rye for us — and there's a big cake of salt for the Red Buck, and there's vegetables, all kinds of vegetables out of the garden, all fresh and washed clean, no dirt on *them*, and there's clover and there's bluegrass and buckwheat. There's even nuts for the squirrels and chipmunks — and they're all starting in to eat them now, Mole, and if you don't mind — if you'll excuse me — I think I'll sort of join in."

Willie joined in with his cousins, who were fairly wallowing in grain. Near by, Uncle Analdas, looking slightly bewildered, was gulping alternate mouthfuls of clover and carrots. Porkey was working determinedly on a pile of buckwheat, unconscious that a sprig of it, draped over one ear, gave him a most rakish appearance.

There was a steady sound of chewing and munching and

champing. The Folks sat silent, the glow of the Man's pipe rising and falling with slow regularity, the Lady gently rubbing Mr. Muldoon's jowls. The Red Buck licked salt till his lips were thick with foam, took a long drink from the pool, and then, tossing his head, snorted loudly. The eating stopped and Willie eased his belt a hole or two; his softly furred little stomach seemed to have suddenly swollen alarmingly.

With slow and stately tread the Red Buck began a circuit of the garden. The Doe and their Fawn walked behind him. Obediently all the other Animals fell into line. There came Phewie and the Gray Fox, side by side, waddling Porkey and Uncle Analdas, Mother and Father with Little Georgie between them, his arms around their necks, the Pheasant and his wife, with their mincing, rocking-chair walk, feathers glimmering bronze-gold in the moonlight.

[124]

There came all the Fieldmouse tribe, the Raccoon and the
Opossum, the Chipmunks and the Squirrels, gray and red.
And alongside them, on the very edge of the garden, the
quivering and humping of the earth showed the progress
of the Mole and his three stout brothers.

Slowly, solemnly the procession circled the garden until
they had all returned to the little lawn where the Good
Saint stood. The Red Buck snorted again, and all gave
attention as he spoke.

"We have eaten their food." His voice rang out impres-
sively. "We have tasted their salt, we have drunk their
water, and all are good." He tossed his proud head in the
direction of the garden. "From now on this is forbidden

ground." His chisel-sharp hoof rapped the earth. "Does any-one dispute me?"

None did, and there was a silence, broken at last by the voice of Uncle Analdas. "Haow 'bout them dingblasted Cut-worms?" he called. "They don't know no laws or decent regulations."

The Mole, who had been a little slower than the rest, leaned his elbows on the earth as he reared up from his just-completed tunnel and turned his blind face toward the sound. "We'll patrol," he said, smiling, "me and my brothers, night and day, turn and turn about. Good hunting too; got six on that trip."

As the Animals resumed their dining, Phewie and the Gray Fox suddenly pricked up their ears at a clatter from the grape arbor back of the house. Sulphronia's mellow voice echoed up the Hill. "Hi, Mr. Skunk," she called, "come and get it." Eagerly they trotted away into the darkness.

The moon was dipping behind the Pine Wood before the last trace of the feast was cleaned up and the well-stuffed Little Animals took their way down the Hill. They scat-tered to their respective homes with gay but sleepy farewells. Mother carried a small market basket on either arm. "Soup tomorrow," she cried happily. "Peavine and lettuce soup, tomorrow and every day from now on."

Uncle Analdas cleared his throat. "If there ain't nobody occupying that there guest room," he announced a little sheepishly, "I might sorta try it out again fer a spell. Porkey's a good feller and all that, but that there burrow of his is mighty musty, yes *sir*, mighty musty, and as fer his cookin' — "

"Of course you shall, Uncle Analdas." Mother smiled. "Your room is just as you left it. I've dusted it every day."

Little Georgie, running in gay circles, called to Father. "Any new Dogs around?"

"I understand there is a newly arrived pair of Setters up on Good Hill Road," Father answered. "Said to be very highly bred and quite capable. When you have had a few more days of rest and recuperation we must give them a workout."

"I'm ready any time," laughed Little Georgie gaily. "Any time at all." He leaped high in the air, rapping his heels together three times, soared clear over Father, Mother, *and* Uncle Analdas. "I'm *fine!*"

Each evening throughout the summer the kindly Saint's ledge was spread with a banquet; each morning it was clean and neatly swept. Each night the Red Buck, Phewie, and the Gray Fox patrolled the premises against wandering marauders, the Mole and his stout brothers made their faithful rounds.

All summer Mother and the other womenfolk preserved, packed, and put away winter stores. Once again there were parties and merrymaking, laughter and dancing. Good days had come back to the Hill.

Tim McGrath surveyed the flourishing garden and lifted his voice in wonderment. "Louie," he said, "I just can't understand it. Here's these new folks with their garden and not a sign of a fence around it, no traps, no poison, no nothing; and not a thing touched, not a thing. Not a footprint onto it, not even a cutworm. Now me, I've got all them things, fences, traps, poisons; even sat up some nights with a shotgun—and what happens? All my carrots gone and half my beets, cabbages et into, tomatoes tromp down, lawn all tore up with moles. Fat-Man-down-to-the-Crossroads, he keeps dogs even and he ain't got a stalk of corn left standing, all his lettuce gone, most of his turnips. I can't understand it. Must just be Beginner's Luck."

"Must be," agreed Louie. "Must be that—or something."

UP DANBURY way

FAT-MAN-AT-THE-CROSSROADS

THE NORTH FIELD

THE

THE PINE WOOD

PORKEY'S HOME